Little women

小婦人

Louisa May Alcott

Retold and Activities by Silvana Sardi
Illustrated by Júlia Sardà

The Commercial Press

Contents 目錄

故事錄音開始和結束的標記

start ▶   **stop** ■

Mrs. Margaret March   Meg

Jo   Amy   Beth

Reading Comprehension (Preliminary)

1 **Read about *Little Women*. Complete the text with the correct word for each space from A, B, C or D.**

Little Women is a book about family .....*B*..... . The story is about four sisters (**1**) .... grow up in a poor family and are always trying to find ways to (**2**) .... some money. Their father is away at war, so the four girls try and help their mother as (**3**) .... as they can. The girls have all got very different characters. Meg the (**4**) .... , is sixteen years old and is very pretty. She helps the family (**5**) .... teaching children. Jo, on the other hand, is tall and slim and often acts more like a boy She looks (**6**) .... an old lady but doesn't find it very interesting. Beth, 13 years old, is the quietest of them (**7**) .... She's shy and peaceful and most of the (**8**) .... lives in a world of her own. Amy, the youngest, is also the (**9**) .... beautiful and she knows it! With her blue eyes and long, blond, curly hair, she feels very important and always acts like a young lady. (**10**) .... all these differences and all their problems, Mrs. March manages to keep the family together.

	A	B	C	D
	A parents	B life	C relationship	D house
1	A which	B whose	C who	D where
2	A earn	B do	C arrange	D involve
3	A many	B lots	C few	D much
4	A most old	B elder	C older	D eldest
5	A with	B by	C at	D for
6	A for	B at	C to	D after
7	A all	B every	C each	D both
8	A days	B hours	C time	D period
9	A such	B much	C most	D very
10	A unless	B anyway	C but	D despite

Vocabulary

2 **Complete the sentences with a time expression from the box.**

> ~~yesterday~~ • tomorrow • before • so far
> after • during • as soon as

...*Yesterday*... I went out and bought a new pullover.

1 Sara has only read two pages of her book ....

2 .... leaving, they checked they had closed all the windows.

3 I'll call you .... I arrive.

4 Their house was damaged .... the storm.

5 .... eating, they tidied up the kitchen.

6 Jane's cousin is arriving on the 7 o' clock train ....

Listening

▶ 2 **3** **Listen to the start of Chapter One and decide if these sentences are true (T) or false (F).**

	T	F
The girls are talking about Christmas.	☐	☐
1 Meg would like to be rich.	☐	☐
2 The girls will receive lots of presents at Christmas.	☐	☐
3 Their mother is with their father.	☐	☐
4 Jo likes reading.	☐	☐
5 Amy is the artist of the family.	☐	☐
6 Their father has always been poor.	☐	☐

Chapter 1

Christmas Time

▶2 "I hate being poor when it's Christmas," complained Meg, looking down at her old dress.

"I know; Christmas without presents just won't be the same," said Jo.

"It's not fair that other girls have lots of nice things," said Amy sadly.

"But we've got father and mother and each other," said Beth, quietly from her corner.

All four girls were sitting around the fire in the living room. They were waiting for their mother to come home. Their father was away at war like many others.

"Father won't be with us," said Meg. "Marmee[1] says that this is going to be a hard winter for everybody, especially for all the soldiers in the army. That's why we must forget about presents."

For a moment, they all thought about what they wanted for Christmas. They each had a dollar. Jo wanted a new book; Meg, something pretty to wear; Beth, some new music for her piano; Amy, some new pencils to draw with. Their father had

1. Marmee: 媽媽

been a rich man once, but had lost all his money when the girls were still little.

"I'd love to go and fight with papa, instead of staying here and knitting socks for the army," said Jo.

"Oh Jo!" said Beth, laughing. "You're more like a brother than a sister to us, so we need you here to protect us."

They all laughed, then suddenly, Amy looked at the clock on the wall above the fire and saw that it was 6 o'clock. The girls immediately forgot all their worries and Beth put her mother's slippers[1] near the fire. "Marmee really needs new slippers; these ones are so old," she said.

"I'll buy her new slippers for Christmas," said Jo immediately.

"No, I will, I'm the eldest," said Meg.

"Why don't we all buy her something instead of a present for ourselves?" suggested Beth.

"What a wonderful idea, Beth!" said the others all together.

"I'll buy her some gloves," said Meg.

"I'll get her new slippers," said Jo.

"I want to give her some handkerchiefs," said Beth.

---

1. slippers: 拖鞋

"And I'll give her a little bottle of perfume¹ so I'll have some money left to buy my pencils," said Amy.

The others all laughed. Amy was the youngest so she was allowed to be a little selfish.

It'd be a lovely surprise for their mother. They decided to go shopping the following afternoon. Then the girls started talking about the play they were preparing for Christmas night. It was a family tradition and they always all had fun. When Mrs. March arrived that evening, she found her four lovely daughters chatting² happily around the fire.

That night she had a special surprise for them, a letter from their father. It was full of stories about camp life, but he never complained once about anything. Everyone cried at the end and missed him even more.

"I'll try and not be wild, and be what he loves to call me, 'a little woman', and do my duty here," said Jo.

Before going to bed, Beth played the old piano and they all sang as they did every night.

Christmas morning arrived and Jo woke up first.

---

1. perfume: 香水 ▶PET◀   2. chatting: 閒談 ▶PET◀

She called the others and they went downstairs to see their mother, but she wasn't there.

"She's probably out helping someone," said Hannah, who had lived with them since Meg was born, and was more of a friend than a servant[1] to them all. Just then, Mrs. March came in.

"Merry Christmas, my lovely girls," she said, kissing each of them.

"Where have you been?" asked Jo.

"Near here, there's a mother with six hungry children, and a baby. They have nothing to eat or drink. Will you give them your breakfast, my sweet daughters, as a Christmas present?" asked Mrs. March. She already knew they'd say yes and soon they were all carrying baskets of food over to the unfortunate family. When they arrived at the Hummel's poor house, Hannah made a fire and the girls gave the hungry children the food. Once back home, the girls had bread and milk for their Christmas breakfast, but they were happy, especially when they gave their mother the presents they had bought.

That evening the girls had fun acting for their friends. At the end of the play, Mrs. March

1. servant: 傭人

told them all to come to the kitchen for supper.

Everybody was surprised to see the table full of ice-cream, cakes, biscuits, sweets and chocolates. "When old Mr. Laurence heard what you did for the Hummels, he decided to send you these things," explained their mother.

Mr. Laurence was an old gentleman who lived in the big house next door with his grandson, but they didn't know them very well.

"Remember when the cat ran away and the grandson brought it back?" asked Jo. "We started talking, then he saw Meg coming and walked off.[1] We must try and speak to him, I'm sure he's lonely," she said.

Next morning, Meg and Jo received an invitation to a party on New Year's Eve. Meg was very excited but also worried about Jo's dress. Like hers, it was old, but at least Meg's wasn't burnt at the back. Jo, who didn't care so much, promised to stand against the wall all night. The night of the party, the girls looked very pretty despite their unfashionable clothes. Meg put on high-heeled shoes which hurt her, but she wore them just the same.

1. walked off: 離開

At the party Meg talked to the other girls. Jo stood against the wall. She was bored so found a dark corner to hide in. Suddenly, she realized there was somebody else there. It was the "Laurence boy"! They both laughed and soon they were having fun talking about everybody at the party. Laurie seemed interested in Meg and said how pretty she was. Then, Jo heard Meg calling her. She was sitting on a sofa, holding her ankle. She couldn't walk.

"I knew you'd hurt yourself with those shoes. Now, how am I going to get you home?" said Jo.

"Don't worry," said Laurie, "I'll take you home in my grandfather's carriage[1]."

"Oh no, it's so early! You can't want to leave the party already," said Meg.

"Don't worry, I always go home early," said Laurie.

So that night, the girls went home in a beautiful carriage; the perfect end to a brilliant evening.

Next day, however, both girls had to go back to work; Meg to the four spoilt children she taught, and Jo to Aunt March, who was always in a bad mood.

1. carriage: 馬車

After-reading Activities

Stop & Check

1 **Match the sentences to the person who said them. Then, put them in order (1 to 7) as they happen in Chapter One.**

6		Merry Christmas, my lovely girls. ————— Marmee
☐	**A**	I'll buy her some gloves.
☐	**B**	Don't worry, I always go home early.
☐	**C**	She's probably out helping someone.
☐	**D**	Why don't we all buy her something instead of a present for ourselves?
☐	**E**	I'd love to go and fight with papa, instead of staying here and knitting socks for the army.
☐	**F**	And I'll give her a little bottle of perfume so I'll have some money left to buy my pencils.

Amy

Beth

Jo

Meg

Laurie

Hannah

Grammar

2 **Complete the sentences with the comparative form of the adjectives given.**

Meg would like a (pretty) .....*prettier*..... dress than the one she's wearing.

1 Amy is a bit (selfish) .... than her sisters.

2 The Hummels were (hungry) .... than the girls on Christmas morning.

3 Meg was (excited) .... than Jo about the party invitation.

4 Laurie lives in a (big) .... house than the girls.

5 Meg's job is (bad) .... than Jo's.

6 Meg's dress was (good) .... than her sister's.

Writing

3a **Write four short descriptions of the sisters, Meg, Jo, Beth and Amy. Talk about:**

- their character
- their hobbies and interests

3b **Now say which sister you prefer and why.**

....

....

....

....

Pre-reading Activity

Vocabulary

4 **Read the definitions and complete the words which all appear in Chapter Two.**

	A place with plants and flowers.	_g a r d e n_
1	Something sweet to eat, usually made with flour.	c_ _ _
2	A person you don't know.	s _ _ _ _ _ _ _
3	The person who lives in the house next to yours.	n _ _ _ _ _ _ _
4	A talking bird.	p _ _ _ _ _
5	A place full of books.	l _ _ _ _ _ _
6	A short written message.	n _ _ _

Chapter 2

Good Neighbours

▶ 4 One snowy day, Jo went out to the garden to clean the path. The Marches' old, brown house was next to Mr. Laurence's, with a low wall separating the two gardens. Jo often thought that the Laurence house was tidier and more beautiful than theirs, but too quiet. She hadn't seen Laurie since the party and wondered if he ever felt lonely in that big house. Then, looking up, she saw him at the upstairs window. He seemed sad so she made a little snowball, and threw it at Laurie's window. The boy smiled and opened the window.

"Hey, are you sick?" shouted Jo.

"I'm better now, thank you. I've had a bad cold and haven't been out for a week."

"I'm sorry. What do you do all day?"

"Nothing, I'm so bored."

"Does nobody come and visit you?"

"No. Will you come?"

"If mother will let me. I'll go and ask her. Close the window and wait for me. I'll be back soon."

Jo ran to look for her mother, who happily said

yes. A minute later, Jo was in Laurie's room with a cake from Meg and Beth's kittens to play with.

"I often see you all sitting around the fire in the evening with your mother," said Laurie. "She seems so sweet." He was silent for a moment then said: "You know, I haven't got a mother."

Jo felt sorry for him and said: "Instead of looking at us through the window, you must come and visit. Everybody would love to meet you! Wouldn't your grandpa let you?"

"I think so. It's just that he doesn't want me to bother[1] strangers," said Laurie.

"We aren't strangers, we're your neighbours, and you wouldn't bother us at all," said Jo.

"Grandpa isn't bad; he just lives among his books. Then, there's Mr. Brooke, my teacher, but he doesn't stay here, so I'm usually at home on my own."

"Well, that's no good,[2] you ought to go out more. Forget about being shy," said Jo in her usual direct way. Laurie smiled, happy to have this new friend. Jo told him about Aunt March, with her talking parrot and spoilt dog. She also discovered that Laurie loved books like her.

---

1. **bother:** 麻煩   2. **that's no good:** 那不太好

"Come and see our library," said Laurie. "You needn't be afraid, Grandpa is out."

"I'm not afraid of anything," said Jo laughing.

The library was a lovely room full of books, pictures and statues[1]. Laurie left Jo alone there for a moment to speak to his doctor. While she was looking at a big picture of Laurie's grandpa on the wall, she heard the door opening behind her. Without turning, she said: "I'm sure I shouldn't be afraid of your grandpa, he's got kind eyes."

"Thank you, madam," said a man's voice. It was Laurie's grandfather! Jo turned, her face red. For once[2], she didn't know what to say.

"So, you're not afraid of me, hey?"

"Not much, sir."

"So, you like me!" said the old man laughing. Jo relaxed and began to chat happily.

"You're like your grandfather, young girl. He was a kind, honest man. Tell your mother I'll come and see her one day," said Mr. Laurence.

Jo certainly would, and she couldn't wait to tell her sisters all about her special day at the Laurence's.

A few days later, Mr. Laurence came to see Mrs. March and they became good neighbours. He said

---

1. statues: 雕像 ▶PET◀   2. For once: 這一次

that her girls could come and visit any time as he was happy Laurie had such good friends.

Meg loved walking in his garden; Jo loved his library; Amy tried to copy his pictures; only Beth was too shy to go to the house. Then, one day, Mr. Laurence came and asked Beth if she would come and play his piano sometimes, since Laurie didn't want to play anymore.

Beth was so excited that she forgot to be shy, and putting her small hand in his, walked to his house.

"I had a little girl once, with eyes like yours," said Mr. Laurence, as he led Beth to the piano.

After that, Beth went to play every day and forgot to be afraid. Weeks later, she decided to make slippers for the old man to thank him. When they were finished, she left them in his study with a short, simple note. Two days later, a piano arrived for Beth with this letter:

> *"Dear Madam,*
> *My slippers are beautiful. This piano once*
> *belonged to the little granddaughter I lost.*
> *I want you to have it now. Your friend,*
> *James Laurence."*

To everyone's surprise, shy, little Beth went straight to Mr. Laurence in his study[1]. Remembering the little girl he had lost, she put her arms around his neck and kissed him on the cheek[2]. The old man was so pleased that he sat her on his knee, and feeling as if he had found his granddaughter again, they talked together until it was time for her to go home.

While Beth had made a new friend, Amy wasn't happy at all. First, her teacher had been angry with her for eating sweets in class. Then, one Saturday afternoon, Amy saw Meg and Jo getting ready to go out.

"Where are you going?" she asked.

"Little girls shouldn't ask questions," answered Jo.

"Oh Meg, please tell me! I'm bored and want to come too," said Amy.

"I'm sorry Amy. I can't tell you. It's a secret," said Meg kindly.

Laurie had invited the girls to the theatre and Jo wanted to have fun, not look after Amy.

"Look Amy," said Jo angrily, "you're too young to come with us."

1. **study:** 書房　　　　　2. **on the cheek:** 在臉頰上

Then Laurie arrived and as the two girls left, Amy shouted:

"You'll be sorry for this, Jo!"

Jo didn't realize how serious her sister was, until the next day.

Jo sat down at her desk to write another story in her little book, but couldn't find it. She had written three short stories so far and wanted to finish the book for her father's return. She looked in the drawer – nothing. Then she remembered Amy's words. She ran downstairs shouting:

"Amy, where's my book?"

"I don't know and I don't care!" said Amy.

"Don't tell lies, Amy. What have you done with it?"

"I burnt it in the fire last night," said Amy.

Jo had never felt so angry. She shook Amy hard[1], saying:

"I'll never forgive you for this!"

Meg ran to help Amy, while Beth went to Jo. That evening, Amy tried to say she was sorry, but Jo refused to speak to her. Jo was so like her mother.

Mrs. March used to get angry a lot when she was a girl, but over the years she had learned to

---

1. **shook sb hard**: 猛力搖動某人

control herself, and now, instead of shouting, she kept her lips shut tight.

Next day, Jo decided to go skating[1] on the frozen river with Laurie. Amy followed her because she still wanted Jo to forgive her. At the river, Jo saw Amy coming, but she didn't wait for her. Laurie was in front and said:

"Don't go skating in the middle, the ice is too thin."

Jo heard him, but Amy didn't. She was still too far away. Then, there was a terrible scream. Jo turned and saw Amy in the middle of the river. The ice was breaking and Amy was disappearing into the water below. Jo was so frightened, she couldn't move. Luckily, Laurie was there. He pulled Amy out of the icy water and they got her home before she froze to death. That night, Jo held her little sister until Amy fell asleep. Then, Jo cried in her mother's arms, while Mrs. March kissed Jo's pale, worried face and told her everything would be alright.

1. **skating:** 溜冰 ▶PET◀

After-reading Activities

Stop & Check

1 Choose the best answer A, B or C about Chapter Two.

Jo goes to visit
Laurie in
A ☑ winter.
B ☐ summer.
C ☐ spring.

1 Mr. Laurence's
house is
A ☐ big and brown.
B ☐ small and tidy.
C ☐ big and quiet.

2 Jo sees Laurie
A ☐ at the door.
B ☐ at the window.
C ☐ on the garden
wall.

3 Laurie lives
A ☐ with his
grandfather.
B ☐ on his own.
C ☐ with his
teacher.

4 In the past,
Mr. Laurence had
known
A ☐ Jo's aunt.
B ☐ Jo's grandpa.
C ☐ Jo's father.

5 Beth decides to give
Mr. Laurence
A ☐ some piano music.
B ☐ her kittens.
C ☐ something to wear.

6 Beth reminds Mr. Laurence
of his
A ☐ granddaughter.
B ☐ daughter.
C ☐ sister.

7 Amy had problems at school
because
A ☐ she didn't want to
share her sweets.
B ☐ she ate some sweets
during the lesson.
C ☐ she went to the theater
instead of school.

8 Laurie invites Meg and Jo to
A ☐ the theatre.
B ☐ to go skating.
C ☐ to swim in the river.

9 Amy almost dies because
A ☐ she burns herself with
the fire.
B ☐ she walks all the way
to the theatre.
C ☐ she falls into icy water.

Grammar

2 Choose the best answer.

Mrs. March let Jo (go)/to go and visit Laurie.

1 Laurie came to see the girls instead of *stay/staying* at home on his own.

2 Laurie's grandpa didn't want him *to bother/bother* strangers.

3 Laurie ought *go/to go* out more and talk to people.

4 Jo needn't *to be/be* afraid of Mr. Laurence because he's a kind man.

5 Jo couldn't wait *to tell/tell* her sisters about Mr. Laurence and his house.

6 Mr. Laurence decided *giving/to give* Beth a piano.

Pre-reading Activity

Listening

▶ 5 **3 Listen to the start of Chapter Three and decide if these sentences are true (T) or false (F).**

	T	F
It was summer now.	☐	☑
1 Meg's friend was coming to stay for two weeks.	☐	☐
2 Mrs. March had bought her daughter fashionable gloves.	☐	☐
3 The Moffat family had a lot of money.	☐	☐
4 The Moffat family never had parties.	☐	☐
5 Meg got flowers from Laurie.	☐	☐
6 Meg wrote a note to her mother.	☐	☐

Chapter 3

Lazy Days

▶ 5 It was spring, and Meg was excited about staying with her friend, Annie Moffat, for two weeks. Mrs. March had bought her daughter new gloves and a green umbrella for the occasion[1].

"I'm so lucky to have all these new things," said Meg, "even if they aren't the latest fashion."

When it was time to go, Mrs. March kissed her eldest daughter goodbye. She hoped Meg wouldn't come back with her head full of silly ideas. The Moffats were, after all, very rich and fashionable.

The Moffat's house was indeed beautiful and, at first, Meg felt a bit nervous. However, the people were kind, and she soon began to enjoy the lazy days full of parties and fun. It was very different from her usual simple life at home. The more she saw Annie Moffat's pretty things, the more she wanted them.

One evening, the girls were getting ready for a party, when some flowers arrived for Meg. They were from Laurie.

1. occasion: 場合 ▶PET◀

"Who are the flowers from, Meg?" asked the girls excitedly.

"Laurie, and there's a note from Mother too," said Meg.

6 The others looked at each other and laughed. They obviously thought Laurie was much more than just a simple friend for Meg. Everybody at the party wanted to know who the "fresh girl with the beautiful eyes" was. Meg was a big success with her simple ways and appearance. Later, she went into the garden for some air. The Moffat girls were there and she heard one say:

"Mrs. March has planned well, hasn't she? Laurie will make a good husband for Meg and the family will solve their money problems too."

Meg's face turned red. She was both angry and ashamed. She went back into the house before they noticed her. She wanted to cry but did her best to seem happy until the evening ended.

The following Thursday, the Moffats had another party. This time, they invited Laurie. Meg had tried to explain that he was just a friend, but the girls didn't believe her. They gave her a tight dress to wear and did her hair[1] and make-up. When they had finished, there was nothing of the old, simple Meg left.

"You're a little beauty," they said. Meg believed she was like a real lady until Laurie saw her.

"What have you done?" asked Laurie "You're like a painted doll!"

At first, Meg was angry, then she realized he was right.

"Please, don't tell them at home, Laurie. Mother would be so disappointed in me."

"Don't worry, I won't say a word," said Laurie. "Come on! Let's get some lemonade!"

"Yes, let's!" said Meg, happy to have her old friend again. When Saturday came, Meg was ready to go back home to her simple, happy family life.

That evening, Meg told her mother about the party, and what she had heard the Moffats say.

"Meg, it's normal to like nice things," said her mother. "Just remember, there are more important things in life, like love and respect. And forget what they said about Laurie. Of course, I have plans for my daughters. I want you all to have a happy life, either married or single; that's my

---

1. **did her hair:** 梳理她的頭髮

plan." With these words, she kissed her daughter goodnight, and Meg felt safe and loved.

The girls loved games, and they had had a secret club, called the "Pickwick Club", for a year. Now that Laurie had become a good friend, he too became part of the club. On his first evening as a member, Laurie had a surprise for them.

"To thank you all, I have made a private post-office in the garden shed[1]. It used to be full of stuff[2] for the garden and old chairs, but now it's empty and clean."

"Wow! What a great idea!" said the girls.

"I know!" said Laurie, laughing. "We can leave letters, books and any other stuff to send each other. Here are the keys. One for the Marches and one for the Laurences."

The post-office soon became an important part of their daily lives. Lots of different stuff passed betwcen the two houses; long letters, poetry and music. Even old Mr. Laurence liked it and sent funny notes, while his gardener sent a love-letter to Hannah. They all laughed at this, not realizing how many love-letters the little post-office would hold in the future.

---

1. **shed:** 小木屋　　　　2. **stuff:** 物品 ▶PET◀

31

Summer came, and Jo and Meg were glad that they didn't have to work for the next three months.

"I'm going to get up late every morning and do nothing all day," said Meg.

"I'm going to read and have fun with Laurie," said Jo.

"Let's not do any lessons Beth, and play all the time," said Amy.

"Well, I will, if Marmee doesn't mind," said Beth. "There are lots of new songs I want to learn."

Mrs. March was in a corner of the room listening to her girls. "You can do what you want for a week and see how you like it," she said. "But I think you'll find 'all play and no work' as bad as 'all work and no play'."

"Never!" said the girls.

"We'll see," said their mother quietly.

Of course, Mrs. March was right. After a few days, things started to go wrong. Jo had a headache[1] because she had read too much; Beth's pet bird died because she forgot to feed it; Amy got bored drawing on her own, and Meg slept so late that she missed breakfast and had to eat on her own which she didn't like at all.

---

1. **headache:** 頭痛

On Saturday, Mrs. March decided to stay in bed all day, and Hannah went on holiday. When the girls got up, there was no fire in the kitchen and no breakfast.

"Hannah and I have worked hard all week doing your jobs," said their mother. "Now, you can do everything."

Jo decided to take control of[1] the kitchen and make lunch for everyone. What a mistake! She also invited Laurie and Miss Crocker, a poor old lady who lived nearby. Mrs. March went out for lunch. Of course, the food was terrible. Jo hoped her strawberry dessert would save the day, but she had put salt on the strawberries instead of sugar! They were so disgusting[2] that Amy ran away from the table. Poor Jo's face went bright red and she wanted to cry. Then, Laurie laughed and soon they were all laughing.

That evening, Mrs March said:

"Do you want another week of lazy days or have you had enough, my dear girls?

"No, give us back our old duties, please," said the girls and Mrs. March laughed happily.

---

1. **take control of:** 控制   2. **disgusting:** 令人厭惡

One morning, Beth came in from their post-office with a letter for Meg from Mr. Brooke and one of her gloves. He had written the words of a German song she wanted.

"I wonder where the other glove is," said Meg, not thinking for a moment that maybe Mr. Brooke had found both but kept one. Mrs. March looked at her pretty daughter, but said nothing.

The following day, the girls spent the whole day with Laurie and some English friends who had come to visit him. They all enjoyed themselves. They had a picnic, then played some games. Mr. Brooke spent most of the day talking to Meg. He even defended[1] her against the unkind words of the English girl, Kate, who, on hearing that Meg taught children, said:

"In England, it isn't nice for a woman to work."

"Young ladies in America are respected for making money for themselves," said Mr. Brooke.

Meg was grateful to him and smiled. Mr. Brooke seemed very different to her today; not serious and boring as she had once thought, but pleasant and kind.

1. **defended:** 保護

After-reading Activities

Stop & Check

1 Answer the questions about Chapter Three.

How did Meg pass the time at the Moffat's?
She went to parties and had fun.

1 Why was Mrs. March worried about Meg?
2 Why did the Moffats invite Laurie to the second party?
3 Why was Laurie surprised when he saw Meg at the party?
4 What did Laurie make in his garden for them to use?
5 Why did nobody like Jo's dessert?
6 What did Mr. Brooke keep that belonged to Meg?

Preliminary - Writing

2 Complete the second sentence so that it means the same as the first. Use no more than 3 words.

The Marches haven't got as much money as the Moffats.
The Moffats are ......*richer*...... than the Marches.

1 Both Jo and Laurie love reading.
Jo loves reading as .... Laurie.
2 While she was at the Moffat's house, Meg went to parties.
Meg went to parties .... her two weeks at the Moffat's house.
3 The girls had had the Pickwick club for a year.
The girls started the club a ....
4 Amy can draw very well.
Amy is .... drawing.
5 Amy didn't like drawing by herself.
Amy hated drawing on ....
6 Mr. Brooke looked forward to seeing Meg at the picnic.
Mr. Brooke .... to see Meg at the picnic.

Grammar

3 Complete the sentences with a question tag.

The Moffat family have got a beautiful house, _haven't they_?

1 Mrs. March will be glad when Meg comes home again, ...?

2 Laurie wasn't pleased when he saw Meg at the party, ...?

3 The post-office became important to them all, ...?

4 Jo had never cooked before, ...?

5 Mrs. March knows her daughters well, ...?

6 Mr. Brooke would love to talk to Meg all day, ...?

Pre-reading Activity

Vocabulary

4 Complete the sentences about Chapter Four with a verb from the box. Remember to put the verb in the correct form.

> waste • argue • speak • sell • keep • go • write

In their new society, the girls ...._keep_.... busy outside because it's still warm.

1 They all .... about their dreams while they're sitting together at the top of the hill.

2 Sometimes Laurie is lazy and .... his time, instead of doing something useful.

3 Mr. Brooke often .... with Laurie because the boy doesn't study enough.

4 Jo .... two stories and takes them to a newspaper.

5 Jo .... her hair and earns some money for her family.

6 Mrs. March .... to Washington because her husband is ill.

Chapter 4

Busy Bees

▶7 One September afternoon, Laurie saw the girls walking up the hill behind their house. They were all wearing big hats. He was bored so he decided to follow them. When he got to the top, the girls were already busy. Amy was drawing, Beth was picking flowers, and Meg and Jo were knitting socks for the army.

"What's happening here today?" asked Laurie. "And why wasn't I invited?"

"Hey Laurie!" said Jo. "This is the 'Busy Bee Society'. We didn't tell you about it because we thought you might laugh at us."

"Why should I laugh? At least you're doing something useful, instead of wasting the afternoon arguing with people," said Laurie.

"You haven't argued with poor Mr. Brooke, have you?" asked Meg.

"Yes, with him, and with my grandfather. Everybody wants me to go to college[1]," said Laurie.

"Come and sit down and look at our land of dreams," said Beth kindly.

1. college: 大學 ▶PET◀

"How beautiful your land of dreams is," said Laurie, looking at the green fields and hills on the other side of the river.

"I have lots of dreams," said Laurie. "First, I'd like to see the world. Then, I'd like to become a famous musician. Instead, Grandfather wants me to continue his business but I hate ships. I think I'll have to run away, like my father did."

"I'm sure that if you do well at college, your grandfather will let you do what you want," said Meg. "My dream is to have a lovely house full of pretty things and lots of servants."

"I'd have lots of horses, and I'd write books and become rich and famous," said Jo.

"I'd stay at home with Father and Mother, and help take care of the family," said Beth.

"My biggest dream is to be the best artist in the whole world," said Amy.

They all laughed and ran back down the hill for tea. For the moment, their dreams were just castles in the air[1].

One October afternoon, Jo put some papers in her pocket and went out. She walked quickly along the road until she came to a tall building

1. castles in the air: 空中樓閣

with a dentist's sign outside. She looked around, then walked up the stairs.

She didn't see Laurie on the other side of the road. He was sure she was going to get a tooth out and decided to wait for her. Jo appeared ten minutes later.

"Are you alright? Why did you go alone?" asked Laurie.

"I didn't want anybody to know," said Jo.

"How many did he take out?"

"Eh?" Then, Jo laughed and said: "Two need to come out, but I must wait a week. Anyway, what were you doing here, Laurie?"

"Just talking to Ned Moffat."

"Humph[1]! I don't like that boy," complained Jo.

"Never mind Ned; tell me your secret, Jo."

"You won't say anything about it at home, will you, Laurie?"

"Of course not!"

"Well, I've written two stories and the newspaper will let me know if they like them next week."

"Brilliant!" shouted Laurie.

"So that's my secret. Now what's yours?" asked Jo.

"I know where Meg's glove is."

1. Humph: 哼

"Where?"

"In Mr. Brooke's pocket!"

"That's terrible!" said Jo.

"No, it's romantic," said Laurie.

"Well, I don't want anybody to take Meg away!"

"You'll feel better about it when somebody comes to take you away."

"No I won't!" said Jo angrily, and leaving Laurie behind, she ran all the way home.

Two weeks later, Meg saw Jo running around the garden with a newspaper in her hand. Laurie was trying to catch her. Then, they both stopped and laughed together for a long time.

"What will we do with that girl? She'll never learn to behave like a young lady," said Meg.

"I like her the way she is; she's so funny," said Beth.

Then, Jo came in and sat on the sofa with the newspaper in front of her.

"Anything interesting?" asked Meg.

"Just a story, nothing much," answered Jo.

"Please, read it to us," said Amy.

Jo began to read and at the end they asked who had written it.

"Your sister," said Jo.

The girls were so proud of Jo that they all started talking at the same time. They didn't know that soon, they'd be even prouder of Jo, and it wouldn't be for another of her stories.

A few days later, the girls were sitting and talking to Laurie when their mother came in with a message in her hand. Her face was very white and they realized there was bad news.

"Oh Marmee, is there something wrong with Father?" asked Jo.

"I'm afraid so. Your father is very ill and is in hospital. I must go to him at once."

Jo was sent to buy some things while Laurie took a letter to Aunt March, asking her for some money for the train journey. Mr. Brooke offered to travel with Mrs. March and she was very grateful. The other girls helped their mother pack. Much later, everything was ready, but Jo hadn't come back yet. Then, the living room door opened and Jo came in. She came over to[1] her mother and gave her twenty-five dollars.

"That's to help bring Father home," said Jo.

"But where did you get the money, Jo?" asked Mrs. March.

---

1. came over to: 來到

Jo said nothing. Instead, she took off her hat to show a head of very short hair.

"Oh my sweet child, you've sold your beautiful hair!" said Mrs. March.

She put her arms around her daughter and held her close, tears running down her face.

"Don't worry, Marmee. Anyway, I was getting too proud of my long hair," said Jo, trying to laugh.

Much later that night, however, Jo cried herself to sleep in the dark.

Early next morning, the girls, Hannah, Laurie and Mr. Laurence were all there to say goodbye to Mrs. March and Mr. Brooke as they started their long journey to Washington. When they had gone, Hannah made coffee for the girls.

"Hope and keep busy; that's what we must do," said Jo. "I'll go as usual to Aunt March and you'll teach the horrible King children, Meg."

"And I'll stay at home with Beth and help her look after the house," said Amy.

When Meg and Jo left to go to work, Beth remembered that her mother always stood at the window to watch them go.

"Look Jo," said Meg, "Little Beth is being mother to us."

"She's such a sweet thing, isn't she?" said Jo.

Mr. Brooke sent them news every day. Their father was still seriously ill, but already seemed a little better now that Mrs. March was there. Each of the girls wrote to their mother in their own way.

Meg chose pretty paper and said how kind Mr. Brooke was to stay in Washington. Jo talked about the time spent with Laurie. Beth sent her mother some flowers she had grown herself. Amy tried to use big words in her letter but ended up making lots of mistakes. However, they all finished their letters in the same way, with lots of love and kisses.

Hannah's letters spoke about how good the girls were, and how they all helped her and each other. Even Mr. Laurence wrote. He told Mrs. March to make good use of Brooke and offered her money if needed.

The girls tried their best to carry on their lives as normally as possible, even if they missed their mother terribly. They could never imagine that more trouble was just around the corner[1] and that they would need to be stronger than ever.

1. around the corner: 臨近

Stop & Check

1 **The following sentences describe what happened in Chapter Four. Put them in the right order (1 to 7).**

A ☐ Mr. Brooke goes to Washington with Mrs. March.
B ☑ Laurie follows the girls one afternoon.
C ☐ The girls write to their mother.
D ☐ Jo sells her hair for twenty-five dollars.
E ☐ Jo reads her story in the newspaper to her sisters.
F ☐ Hannah makes coffee for the girls.
G ☐ Laurie tells Jo where Meg's glove is.

Writing

2a **Imagine you're Meg. Write to Mrs. March while she is in Washington. Talk about:**

- your teaching job with the King children
- how you are managing without her
- how your sisters are

Write about 100 words.

2b **Now imagine you're Jo, writing to her mother. Talk about:**

- looking after Aunt March
- spending time with Laurie
- what you miss about her not being there

Write about 100 words.

....
....
....
....

Grammar

3 Change the sentence from direct to indirect speech.

"I've argued with everybody today," said Laurie.
Laurie said he had argued with everybody that day.

1 "I have lots of dreams," said Laurie.
2 "My biggest dream is to be the best artist in the whole world," said Amy.
3 "I don't like Ned Moffat," said Jo.
4 "I'll go as usual to Aunt March," said Jo.
5 "I must go to your father at once," said Mrs. March.
6 "A newspaper has bought my stories," said Jo.

Pre-reading Activity

Listening

▶ 8 **4 Listen to part of Chapter Five. Choose the correct answer (A, B, or C) for each question.**

How long did the girls behave well?
A For a week.
B For a month.
C For a day.

1 Who wrote to them with good news?
A Their mother.
B Mr. Brooke.
C Their father.

2 Who continued doing all their duties?
A Jo.
B Meg.
C Beth.

3 Jo didn't go to the Hummels because
A she still had a bad cold.
B she wanted to finish writing.
C she had a headache.

4 Beth was worried about the Hummels because
A the baby wasn't well.
B she hadn't seen them for a week.
C Mrs. Hummel didn't have a job.

5 How long did Beth wait for Amy?
A An hour.
B Half an hour.
C An hour and a half.

Chapter 5

Dark Days

▶ 8 The first week, the girls behaved perfectly. Then, as good news arrived from Mr. Brooke, they started to relax and didn't keep quite so busy.

Jo caught a bad cold because she didn't wear a hat. She had to stay at home, and was quite happy lying on the sofa all day, writing. Amy got tired of her house duties and went back to her drawing. When Meg came home after teaching, she wrote long letters to her mother or read Mr. Brooke's letters again and again. Beth was the only one who kept doing all her duties and even some of her sisters'.

Ten days after their mother had left, Beth went to Meg and Jo and said:

"Meg, will you go and see the Hummels, please. You know Marmee said not to forget them."

"I'm too tired," said Meg, who was reading one of Mr. Brooke's letters.

"Can't you go, Jo?" asked Beth.

"Sorry, it's still too stormy for me with my cold," said Jo.

"I thought you were better," said Beth.

"I'm well enough, but I need to finish writing this," said Jo.

"Why don't you go yourself, Beth?" asked Meg.

"I've been every day, but the baby is sick, and I don't know how to help."

"I promise I'll go tomorrow, Beth," said Meg, seeing that her sister was worried.

"I've got a headache and I'm tired. Can't one of you go?" asked Beth again.

"I'm sure Amy will go with you, dear," said Meg. "She'll be home soon."

Beth sat and waited for an hour. Amy didn't come. Nobody noticed as she put on her coat, took some food, and went out in the cold night to visit the Hummels.

9 It was very late when Beth came home. Nobody saw her go upstairs to her mother's room.

Half an hour later, Jo found her with a bottle of medicine in her hand.

"What's the matter Beth?" asked Jo.

Beth put up her hand as if to stop Jo, and said: "You've had scarlet fever[1], haven't you?"

---

1. **scarlet fever:** 猩紅熱

"Yes, years ago, when Meg had it. Why?"

"Oh Jo, the baby's dead!"

"What baby, Beth?"

"The Hummel baby; it died in my arms."

"Oh my poor Beth!" said Jo. "But where was the mother?"

"Mrs. Hummel had gone to get the doctor, but the baby died before she came back. When the doctor arrived, he said that the baby had died of scarlet fever and that another two of the children had it. Then, the doctor looked at me. He told me to go home immediately and to take medicine before I got it too."

"Oh Beth, if anything happens to you, I'll never forgive myself," said Jo.

"My head and my throat hurt and I've got a temperature, but I've taken the medicine so I should be fine," said Beth trying to be brave for her sister.

Jo called Hannah and she took control of the situation. She sent Meg to get the doctor, and told Amy that she would have to go and stay with Aunt March because she hadn't had scarlet fever. Of course, Amy wasn't happy with this arrangement.

Luckily, Laurie was there and promised to come and take her out every day.

"Can I come back as soon as Beth is better?" asked Amy.

"Of course!" said Laurie. "And remember, I'll come every day and tell you how she is."

So, Amy went to stay with Aunt March while her sisters looked after Beth.

The girls thought about telling their mother, but Hannah told them to wait.

"Your mother has enough problems with your father. I'm sure Beth won't be sick for long," she said to Meg and Jo.

Dr. Bangs came and said Beth had scarlet fever, but told her sisters that it didn't seem too serious. Then he went and spoke quietly to Hannah. She turned away so that the girls wouldn't see her worried face.

Meg looked after the house while Jo was a patient and gentle nurse. Beth slept most of the time, and when she was awake, she didn't recognize them anymore.

The days were dark and the girls' hearts were heavy as they felt the shadow of death[1] over their

1. the shadow of death: 死亡陰影

once happy home. Everybody missed Beth; Mr. Laurence, his gardener and cook, and all the other neighbours. Shy, little Beth had lots of friends.

One cold December morning, Doctor Bangs came and, as usual, felt Beth's hot little hand.

"Hannah," he said, "if Mrs. March can leave her husband, then she should come now."

Jo ran to send the message to her mother. She came back to find Laurie with a letter from Mr. Brooke. Their father was getting better, but Jo's heart didn't feel any lighter[1]. Laurie held her in his arms as tears ran down her cheeks.

"Jo, listen to me. Your mother is arriving home tomorrow morning. Grandpa and I couldn't wait any longer and we sent her a message a few days ago," said Laurie.

"What? Mother is coming? Oh Laurie!" said Jo, kissing him, "How can I thank you?"

"By giving me another kiss!" said Laurie laughing. But Jo was already in Beth's room, telling the sleeping child that Marmee was on her way home. This good news brought a breath of fresh air into the house and the girls began to hope again.

1. **lighter:** 輕鬆一些

All that day Beth slept. The doctor came and said that there would probably be some change, soon. Midnight came and went. The girls thought they saw a shadow cross over Beth's white face.

Laurie left to get Mrs. March at the station. It was two o'clock. Jo looked at Beth. It seemed as if there was still no change for the better. An hour later, the doctor arrived.

"The temperature has gone. She's sleeping and breathing normally," he said kindly.

They all laughed and cried together. Then, Mrs. March arrived and their happiness was complete.

During all this time, Amy had been with Aunt March and she couldn't wait to come home. Aunt March gave her lots of duties to do around the house. She had to feed Polly, the parrot, brush the dog, keep the house clean, and do her lessons! She had only one hour for herself, when Laurie came to take her out. In the evening, she had to read to Aunt March until it was time to go to bed.

She missed Meg and Jo terribly[1], and worried about Beth all the time. Ester, the house servant, saw that Amy was unhappy, so she let her play with some jewellery and old dresses.

---

1. **missed sb terribly:** 非常思念某人

One day when Laurie came to visit, Amy was upstairs playing with her aunt's old dresses. He came into the room as she was walking up and down, wearing a big, long green dress and a pink hat. Polly, the parrot, was behind her shouting:

"Aren't we fine, ha-ha!"

"Oh Laurie, how good it is to see you!" said Amy. "That parrot is nothing but[1] trouble. Yesterday, a spider ran under the sofa, and Polly shouted: 'Come out and walk with me, my dear!' That woke Aunt March up, and I had to read to her for the rest of the afternoon! But tell me, Laurie, how is Beth? I miss her so much. I'm so lonely here."

"I'm afraid she's still quite ill," said Laurie, "but don't worry, Amy. Beth is stronger than she seems. I'm sure she'll get better soon."

"Oh, I hope you're right, Laurie," said Amy.

"I'm always right," said Laurie laughing. He wasn't so sure, but he had promised to keep Amy happy, and that's what he would do until she could go back home.

1. **nothing but:** 只會是

Stop & Check

1 Are the following sentences about Chapter Five true (T) or false (F)? Correct the false ones.

	T	F
The girls behaved perfectly for the first month.	☐	☑

They behaved perfectly for the first week.

		T	F
1	Beth took some medicine because she thought she might have scarlet fever.	☐	☐
2	Amy was sent to stay with Aunt March because she was the youngest.	☐	☐
3	The girls didn't want to tell their mother about Beth.	☐	☐
4	Despite being shy, Beth had a lot of friends.	☐	☐
5	Jo was the first to write and tell her mother to come home.	☐	☐
6	Amy had lots of duties to do at her aunt's house.	☐	☐

Grammar

2 Complete the sentences using the correct form of the verb given.

When their father is better, Mrs. March (come) *will come* home.

1 If Mr. Brooke (not write) .... every day, the girls would get worried.

2 When Mrs. March (arrive) .... home, she'll look after Beth.

3 Beth (play) .... the piano if she didn't feel so ill.

4 Amy (not be able) .... to come home until Beth is well again.

5 If Amy didn't do her duties well, Aunt March (not let) .... her go out.

Vocabulary

3 **Complete the sentences with a word from the box.**

> throat • ~~temperature~~ • ill • cold • well • tired • headache

Hannah knew Beth had a ...*temperature*... because her forehead was very hot.

1 Beth couldn't eat anything because her .... hurt.

2 Jo caught a bad .... because she didn't wear a hat when it was stormy.

3 After doing all her duties, Amy felt really .... and went to bed.

4 When the doctor realized how .... Beth was, he told Hannah to tell Mrs. March.

5 Aunt March got a .... when Amy made too much noise.

6 Mr. March still wasn't .... enough to come home.

Pre-reading Activity

Speaking / Writing

4a **What do you think will happen in the last chapter? Work in pairs and talk about the following people.**

Meg   Jo   Mr. Brooke   Laurie

4b **Now use your ideas to write about 35-40 words about the future of each person. Then, after reading chapter six, check and see if you were right.**

Chapter 6

Peaceful Weeks

▶ 10 The first thing Beth saw when she woke up was her mother's sweet face. It was the best medicine ever! Meg and Jo could finally sleep, knowing that Marmee was there to look after little Beth. Laurie went to tell Amy, and even Aunt March cried a little when she heard the good news. Aunt March gave Amy a ring for all her work. Later that day, Mrs. March came to see Amy. They talked and talked and Amy showed her mother the ring.

"Don't you think you're a little too young for an important ring like that, Amy?" asked Mrs. March.

"It's to remind[1] me not to be selfish," said Amy. "Beth isn't selfish and that's why everybody loves her. I want to be loved as much as Beth, so I'm going to do my best to be like her."

"Then wear your ring, my child," said Mrs. March. "And remember that we all love you and miss you. Soon you'll be able to come home," she said as she kissed Amy goodbye.

---

1. **remind:** 提醒 ▶PET◀

58

That evening, Jo told her mother how Mr. Brooke had kept Meg's glove.

"When Laurie saw the glove, Mr. Brooke told him that he liked Meg, but didn't want to say because she was so young and he was so poor." said Jo.

"Do you think Meg likes Mr. Brooke?" asked Mrs. March.

"How should I know?" said Jo. "I know nothing about love and romance. She's still eating and sleeping normally."

"So, do you think Meg isn't interested in John at all?" asked her mother.

"Who?" cried Jo.

"Mr. Brooke," said her mother. "Your father and I started calling him John while we were in the hospital, and he likes it."

"I can imagine!" said Jo angrily. "Now, you'll let him marry Meg just because he was kind to father. He's been very clever, hasn't he?"

"Jo, don't get angry. Mr. Brooke has indeed been very kind and also very honest. He told us about his love for Meg, from the start. He says he wants to have a comfortable home before asking her to marry him and I said that Meg is still too young for now."

Jo wasn't happy at the thought of losing her dear sister to Mr. Brooke, but she promised to say nothing to Meg. Mrs. March promised Jo that Meg would have to wait until she was twenty if she wanted to marry John Brooke, so Jo felt a bit happier. She hated the idea that they were all growing up and that things would change in the family.

Jo spent the next few days with Laurie. Although Jo said nothing, Laurie realized that Mr. Brooke had said or done something about his love for Meg. The boy was a bit annoyed that Mr. Brooke hadn't told him.

Then, Meg began to act in a strange way. She was very quiet and looked worried. Jo was sure Meg was already in love, but her mother told her to just wait and see.

Next day, Jo went to their little post-office in the garden and came back with a letter for Meg. Jo sat back down next to her mother and they continued knitting, when suddenly Meg cried "Ooh!". She was holding the letter in her hand and seemed terribly upset.[1]

1. **upset:** 煩惱

"It's a letter from Mr. Brooke. He says he didn't send me a love letter two days ago and that it was probably a joke. Oh Jo, how could you do this to me?" cried Meg.

"What? I didn't write any letter," said Jo.

In the first letter, Mr. Brooke had said he loved her and wanted to marry her. Meg had answered saying that she could only be his friend for now, and that he should speak to her parents.

"This is all Laurie's work," said Jo as she ran out of the house to get him.

"Don't worry, Meg," said Mrs. March. "There has been no damage done." She then told Meg about John Brooke's true feelings for her.

"Oh Mother, I don't want to think about love yet," said Meg. "If John doesn't know anything about these letters, then tell Jo and Laurie to say nothing."

Then Laurie arrived, and after speaking to Mrs. March alone, he told Meg he was sorry, and that Mr. Brooke knew nothing of[1] the letters. The joke was soon forgotten, but Meg couldn't forget John Brooke quite so easily.

---

1. **knew nothing of:** 完全不知道

The following weeks were peaceful. Beth was now able to lie on the sofa where she played with her cats and dolls. She was still weak but no longer in danger. Mr. March was getting stronger and said he might be home by January. Amy was home now too, and looked at her ring every time she felt she might have a selfish thought.

Christmas Day came, and Laurie and Jo had a surprise for Beth. They took her to the window, and there in the garden was a big snowman[1]. There was music playing, and the snowman held a poem for Beth asking her to accept this gift from Laurie and Jo. Beth loved her special snowman and clapped her hands excitedly at the window. Everyone was happy. Beth was well again. Jo had a new book to read. Mr. Laurence had bought Meg her first silk dress, and Amy had received a beautiful picture for her room. Mrs. March looked at her four daughters and felt proud and happy. It had been a hard year but it had made them all stronger. Suddenly, Laurie's head appeared at the door.

"Here's another Christmas present for the March family," he said excitedly.

1. snowman: 雪人

Then he disappeared, and in his place there were two men. They were both tall. The older man was holding onto the younger man's arm. They stood there, tried to say something, but couldn't. Then, they all ran to each other and kissed, and cried, and laughed. Amy was so excited that she fell over the chair and ended up kissing her father's boots. Mr. Brooke kissed Meg by mistake, or so he said, and Jo danced about the room shouting for joy. Mrs. March kissed her husband, then pointed to the sofa where Beth lay quietly. Mr. March went over to her and held her in his arms. It was the best Christmas ever.

A few days later, Mr. Brooke came back to visit Meg. Jo had spoken to her sister that morning and Meg had said that she had already prepared her speech for Mr. Brooke.

"Don't worry, Jo, you aren't going to lose me yet," said Meg. "I'm going to tell him that I'm too young so we'll just have to stay friends."

"Well done! That's my Meg!" Jo said happily.

But now, Jo wasn't sure that her sister's speech had gone as planned. Meg and Mr. Brooke had been in the living room for ages[1]. She went to

1. **for ages:** 許久

get Brooke's umbrella, to have an excuse to enter the room. She stood at the door for a moment listening. She heard nothing, so opened the door, thinking that Meg had sent him away. What a shock[1] she got! Mr. Brooke was sitting on the sofa with Meg on his knee. He was holding her hand. Jo turned and ran upstairs without saying a word. Mr. and Mrs. March went to speak to the young couple about their plans. Then, Marmee explained the situation to the whole family. They were all happy for Meg now, even Jo! That evening they all ate together. The room was bright with the first romance of the family, and who knows how many others there would be in the future. But that's another story!

1. What a shock: 震驚

Stop & Check

1 Choose the correct words to complete the text about Chapter Six.

Mrs. March arrived just after Beth's temperature came ....*down*....... Meg and Jo were happy that their mother could (**1**) .... after Beth now. Amy was happy to see her mother too and told her about the ring she had decided to wear to (**2**) .... herself not to be selfish. That evening, Jo spoke to her mother about Meg and John Brooke. She didn't think Meg was interested (**3**) .... this young man. Besides, Jo didn't like the idea that they were all (**4**) .... up fast and that the family was changing. Then, Meg got (**5**) .... upset when Laurie sent a letter to her in Mr. Brooke's name. Laurie said he was sorry and promised not to tell (**6**) .... about it. As the weeks passed, Beth (**7**) .... stronger and stronger and didn't have to stay in bed all day anymore. At Christmas, Jo and Laurie (**8**) .... to do something special for Beth and she loved the surprise in the garden. Then there was a surprise for the (**9**) .... family. Mr. Brooke came home with Mr. March on Christmas Day. It was the best Christmas they had ever had.

	A below	**B** down	**C** under	**D** over
1	**A** take	**B** come	**C** look	**D** care
2	**A** remember	**B** remind	**C** say	**D** make
3	**A** in	**B** of	**C** about	**D** to
4	**A** grew	**B** grows	**C** grown	**D** growing
5	**A** really	**B** much	**C** such	**D** enough
6	**A** somebody	**B** anybody	**C** nobody	**D** nothing
7	**A** started	**B** began	**C** got	**D** developed
8	**A** would	**B** might	**C** wanted	**D** used
9	**A** whole	**B** all	**C** most	**D** more

Vocabulary

2 **Complete the crossword about *Little Women*.**

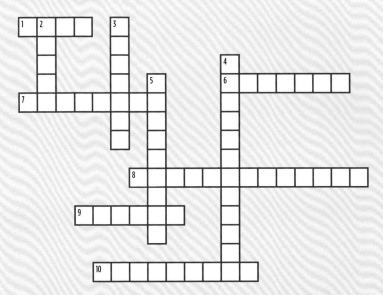

Across

1 On your head. Jo cut hers for money.

6 A place where you can see a play. Amy wanted to go there with Meg and Jo.

7 You take this when you are ill. Beth took some when she came back from the Hummels.

8 Something for your nose. Beth gave her mother these at Christmas.

9 A young cat. Beth liked this animal.

10 A meal. Meg missed having this with the others because she slept late.

Down

2 A part of your body, Meg hurt hers at a party.

3 A hobby, Amy was good at this.

4 Red fruit, Jo spoilt these with salt.

5 Something to read. Jo's story was in one of these.

Louisa May Alcott
(1832 - 1888)

Louisa May Alcott was an American writer, best known for her book *Little Women*, written in 1868.
The book about the March family was so popular that she wrote *Little Women, Part II* also known as *Good Wives* in 1869. Then followed *Little Men* in 1871 and *Jo's Boys* in 1886. These stories of family life have sold millions of copies and have been translated into many languages.

Family Life and Career

Louisa was born in Philadelphia, Pennsylvania, on November 29, 1832. Like the girls in *Little Women*, she and her three sisters knew what it was like to be poor. Her father wasn't good with money and there was often no food in the house. Louisa, like Jo, did all she could to try and help her family. She mended clothes, looked after and taught children, and worked as a cleaner as well. At the age of sixteen, she wrote her first book *Flower Fables*. After this, she tried to run a school but was not very successful.

When the American Civil War broke out, she became a nurse and worked among the soldiers. She wrote their letters for them and tried to make their lives in hospital as comfortable as possible. Her next book, *Hospital Sketches*, which appeared in 1863, told the story of her time spent working in the hospital. Later, she worked for a children's magazine, but she didn't become famous until she wrote *Little Women* two years later. With the money she earned from her books, Louisa Alcott was able to give her mother and sisters a better life, and had the chance to travel the world.

Little Women was written in this house

She believed all people should be free and also fought for a better position for women in society. As she grew older, she had many health problems but still continued to write children's books. She never married, and died in Boston on March 6, 1888, two days after her father's death.

Task

Complete this form about Louisa May Alcott.

Date of Birth:	**1**	....
Place of Birth:	**2**	....
Family:	**3**	....
Jobs done:	**4**	....
Most famous books:	**5**	....
Date of death:	**6**	....

CLIL History
The American Civil War

In the middle of the 19th century, many social changes were happening in America and relationships between the North and the South began to suffer. New industries were developing in the North, while in the South they were still only using the land to grow things like tobacco and cotton. Many people from Africa were brought over to America to work in these fields, even if they didn't want to. They were slaves, that is they were owned by the people they worked for and weren't free to do as they wanted. People in the South became rich by buying and selling slaves and didn't see anything wrong with this kind of business. In the North, however, lots of people wanted the slaves to be free. These people were called *Abolitionists* and included writers like Louisa Alcott. They believed in the *Declaration of Independence* of 1776, which said "All men are created equal" and were ashamed to think that slaves were bought and sold in the South. Therefore, these people created the *Republican Party* and their candidate, Abraham Lincoln, became president. Soon after, South Carolina left the Union of the Northern States. Mississippi followed, then Louisiana, Georgia, Alabama and Florida. In all, eleven Southern states separated from the Union and formed the *Confederate States of America* (*Confederacy*) led by Jefferson Davis in 1861. Civil War broke out on April 12 of that same year. The Northern States (the Union) were led by General Grant and, at first, seemed weaker than the Confederate Army. However, in 1865, after beating the Confederate Army at Gettysburg, the Northern soldiers won the war against the Southerners. They signed for peace in 1865 after 4 years of war, in which many people in both the North and the South lost their lives.

Abraham Lincoln (1809-1865)

Abraham Lincoln was the 16th president of the United States from March 1861 to April 1865 and is considered to be one of the greatest U.S. presidents. Lincoln came from a poor family, but studied hard by himself to become a lawyer. He helped create a more modern society with banks and factories, and made travelling easier with canals and more trains.

He was always against slavery[1] and, during the Civil War, fought to bring the country together again and let slaves be free forever. He abolished[2] slavery officially with the *Thirteenth Amendment to the United States Constitution*. He was shot in the head by John Wilkes Booth, an actor and strong Confederate on April 14, 1865, while he was at the theatre. Lincoln died early the next morning. Hundreds of thousands of people stood and watched the train that took Lincoln's body from Washington D. C. to Springfield, Illinois where he was buried.

1. slavery: 奴隸制
2. abolished: 廢除

Task - Internet search

Find out more about the United States Constitution and describe the following:

- the seven original articles
- the Bill of Rights

Little Women Success over the Years

Little Women was an immediate success when it was first written in 1868. Since then, the story has been used in many forms of entertainment. Let's have a look at some of them.

Little Women at the Cinema

The first two films made about *Little Women* in 1917 and 1918 were silent versions. Then, in 1933 the first 'talking' version was made, starring the famous American actress Katharine Hepburn. She played the part of Jo in the film. The film cost $1 million and took a year to make, with 4,000 people working on it. Like the book, the film was an immediate success and earned more than $100,000 in the first week. Another film was made in 1949, and the most recent, with Winona Ryder and Susan Sarandon, came out in 1994. In this film, Susan Sarandon was Marmee, while Winona Ryder played the part of Jo, and received an *Academy Award Nomination* as Best Actress.

Little Women at the Opera

There is also an opera of *Little Women*, composed in 1998 by Mark Adamo. It was a huge success. Since then, it has been performed not only in the United States, but in countries all over the world, such as Mexico, Japan, Australia, Canada and Belgium.

Little Women on TV

In 1950 and 1958, the BBC showed a six-part series based on *Little Women*. Then, in 1981, a Japanese company, Toei Animation, made an animated television series of *Little Women*. This was followed by another animated version in 1987 by another Japanese company, Nippon Animation. Both series were shown in English on American television.

Little Women: The Musical

Jason Howland wrote the music for this musical based on Louisa Alcott's stories about the March family.

It opened on Broadway at the Virginia Theatre on January 23, 2005 and was repeated 137 times. It then went on tour and covered 30 cities in the United States. The musical was also performed in Sydney, Australia, for a month in 2008.

Task

Answer these questions and then check them with the text.

1 Which film version did Katharine Hepburn star in, and which character did she play?
2 Besides the USA, where else did they perform the musical of *Little Women*?
3 Where were the animated versions of *Little Women* shown in English?
4 Name five countries where the opera version of *Little Women* has been performed.

Test Yourself 自測

Choose A, B, or C to complete the sentences about *Little Women*.

At the start of the story, Meg is wearing
A ☐ a silk dress   B ☑ an old dress   C ☐ her party dress

1 On Christmas night, Mr. Laurence sent the girls
A ☐ nice things to eat   B ☐ nice things to wear   C ☐ nice things to read

2 Jo went to visit Laurie because he had been ill with
A ☐ toothache   B ☐ a bad cold   C ☐ scarlet fever

3 The first time they met, Mr. Laurence said Jo was like
A ☐ her father   B ☐ her grandfather   C ☐ her mother

4 Meg went to say with the Moffats for
A ☐ two weeks   B ☐ two months   C ☐ two days

5 Laurie made a private post-office in the
A ☐ library   B ☐ garden   C ☐ study

6 Laurie's dream was to become
A ☐ an artist   B ☐ a teacher   C ☐ a musician

7 When Jo sold her hair, she got
A ☐ twenty-five dollars   B ☐ thirty dollars   C ☐ fifty dollars

8 When Hannah discovered Beth had scarlet fever, she sent Meg to
A ☐ look for Mr. Laurence   B ☐ call the doctor   C ☐ buy some medicine

9 Polly, the parrot, shouted and woke up Aunt March when she saw
A ☐ a cat   B ☐ a dog   C ☐ a spider

10 Mr. Brooke's first name was
A ☐ Robert   B ☐ John   C ☐ Ned

Syllabus 語法重點和學習主題

//

Verb tenses
Present Continuous: future plans
Past Perfect Simple:
Future with going to and will

Verb forms and patterns
Question tags
Verbs plus infinitive
Verbs plus gerund
Phrasal verbs
Conditional sentences: types 1 and 2
Reported speech
Question words
Active / Passive

Modal verbs affirmative, negative and interrogative forms
Could
Should
Might
Ought to
Have to
Need / needn't
Used to

Clauses
Time clauses introduced by when, while, before, after, as soon as

Answer Key 答案

Little Women

Pages 6-7
1 1 C 2 A 3 D 4 D 5 B 6 D 7 A 8 C 9 C 10 D
2 1 so far 2 Before 3 as soon as 4 during 5 After 6 tomorrow
3 1 T 2 F 3 F 4 T 5 T 6 F

Pages 16-17
1 A Meg B Laurie C Hannah D Beth E Jo F Amy 1 E 2 D 3 A 4 F 5 C 6 X 7 B
2 1 more selfish 2 hungrier 3 more excited 4 bigger 5 worse 6 better
3 personal answers
4 1 cake 2 stranger 3 neighbour 4 parrot 5 library 6 note

Pages 26-27
1 1 C 2 B 3 A 4 B 5 C 6 A 7 B 8 A 9 C
2 1 staying 2 to bother 3 to go 4 be 5 to tell 6 to give
3 1 F 2 F 3 T 4 F 5 T 6 F

Pages 36-37
1 (possible answers)
1 She thought her daughter might come back with silly ideas from the Moffat's.
2 They thought Laurie was Meg's boyfriend and wanted to see them together.
3 Laurie was surprised when he saw Meg at the party because she had changed so much.
4 He made a private post-office for both families to use.
5 Nobody liked her dessert because she had put salt instead of sugar on the strawberries.
6 Mr. Brooke kept one of Meg's gloves.
2 1 so does 2 during 3 year ago 4 very good at 5 her own 6 couldn't wait
3 1 won't she 2 was he 3 didn't it 4 had she 5 doesn't she 6 wouldn't he
4 1 speak 2 wastes 3 argues 4 writes 5 sells 6 goes

Pages 46-47
1 B 1 G 2 E 3 D 4 A 5 F 6 C 7
2a-2b personal answers
3 1 Laurie said he had lots of dreams.
2 Amy said her biggest dream was to be the best artist in the whole world.
3 Jo said she didn't like Ned Moffat.
4 Jo said she would go as usual to Aunt March.
5 Mrs. March said she had to go to their father at once.
6 Jo said a newspaper had bought her stories.
4 1 B 2 C 3 B 4 A 5 A

Pages 56-57
1 1 T 2 F Amy was sent to stay with Aunt March because she hadn't had scarlet fever
3 F The girls wanted to tell their mother about Beth but Hannah stopped them 4 T
5 F Laurie and his grandfather wrote to Mrs. March, telling her to come home, before Jo did 6 T
2 1 didn't write 2 arrives 3 would play 4 won't be able 5 wouldn't let
3 1 throat 2 cold 3 tired 4 ill 5 headache 6 well
4a-4b personal answers

Pages 68-69
1 1 C 2 B 3 A 4 D 5 A 6 B 7 C 8 C 9 A
2 Across 1 hair 6 theatre 7 medicine 8 handkerchiefs 9 kitten 10 breakfast
Down 2 ankle 3 drawing 4 strawberries 5 newspaper